Dedicated To C

Imagine only having a 2nd edition that actually fixes errors.

A (bad) Word From The Author

With **BadMan** I wanted to create something worth the price of admission. I am not massively fond of the way books can create a disconnect between the creator and audience that makes the creator seem untouchable and pretentious. It is because of this that I wanted to create a slightly more informal tone to show that I am very much not untouchable and am just a young novice with a passion project. I also hope that the likes of the colour coded lines and the (bad) additions to titles will demonstrate the level of care and fun I had in creating this and will result in a product with more visible thought put into it than other scripts, largely to make up for the fact that this product is only half of the deal. I've never understood the appeal of paying for a dull script rather than viewing an actual performance so I hope that my efforts in making **BadMan: a very bad play** anything but dull have offset this issue.

PS- Word for the wise, always proof read because it would be quite embarrassing if not...

-Greg Stanage

Big (bad) Bibliography

Apocryphal Adventures
Faux Tale
Smoke and Mirror Memoirs
Illusionary Story
False Memory
Fraudulent Fable
Mendacious Mystery
Counterfactual Chronicles
Pretend Parable
Non-believer Narrative
Allegory for Nothing
Fabricated Experience
A Walk Down A Gaslit Street
Missing Report
Unreliable Legend
Those Past
Were Not Real
Lie R McGee
Lumberjack Does Hollywood
Those Past 2: Were From The future
How'd ya do it?
We're Here We're Beer
Escape From The Complex Complex
Those Past 3: Were From The Future As Well

Table of (bad) Contents

A (bad) Synopsis

In Vermont, **The Director**, a film director with a very high opinion of himself, who has only ever directed B-Movies, is producing a new film *"BadMan"*. He wanders in on an audition for the leading role performed by the eponymous **BadMan**, an absurd and cartoonish villain who has only one goal in life, robbing a bank.

Despite his initial disliking of **Badman, The Director** hires him at the request of the film crew, consisting of the Scottish alcoholic; **Scott L. And**, the inexperienced American; **Alan Bama**, and the posh Englishman; **Richard Heddison**

As production of the film continues **The Director's** patience is tested and broken by the incompetence of his crew all the while **BadMan's** deception and criminal intent is unearthed. Will **BadMan** succeed in his robbery? Or will all of his fiendish lies catch up to him before his payday?

In (a bad) Performance

Key:

Characters and Props are shown in bold. For example "BadMan" and "Bad-Blaster".

[Stage directions are shown in square brackets.]

(Round brackets are used under character names to show how an actor should deliver a line. They may also be used in the middle of a line to show actions that occur while speaking.)

Italics are used for sections of the stage. For example "Stage Right Steps".

Phonetic spelling is used for instances when a character must say a word or name a certain way, for example Richard pronouncing 'Alan' as "Alaan" as well as Scott's slang words such as "dinnae".

1-Staging:

The play was envisioned for a **Proscenium Arch Stage,** specifically one that has a large enough space between the audience and the stage as well as steps leading from the floor up to the stage.

In Acts 1 and 2 the main stage is used as the set at which the characters are creating the film, with a block or chair *Upstage Centre* for **BadMan** to begin his monologue on and a desk *Stage Right* for the crew to converse at, with the space between the stage and audience serving as **BadMan's** lair (the break room which he has modified into *The Bad-Cave*). In front of *Stage Left* there is an assortment of blocks or chairs acting as **BadMan's** car; *The Bad-Mobile*. In front of *Centre Stage* is a flipboard.

During **Act 2** while the curtains are closed, the stage can be modified for **Act** 3 going from a film set to the inside of the bank. The block or chair can be removed from *Upstage Centre* so that the floor would be empty and the film crew can be tied up as hostages. The *Stage Right* desk can have a laptop placed on it so that **BadMan** can deactivate the lasers. The space in front of the stage becomes the outside of the bank with *The Bad-Mobile* staying in place but now being parked outside.

This change can be telegraphed to the audience through the use of signs. With a sign that reads 'The Set' on one side and 'The Bank Down-Town' on the other, the sign can be stationed *Downstage Right* and be flipped by **BadMan** while he goes from the bottom of the *Stage Left Steps* across the space in front of the stage and up the *Stage Right Steps*. Signs can also be used in front of the space in front of the stage with one side reading 'The Bad-Cave' and the other side reading 'The Outside of The Bank Down-Town'.

2-Props:

Any props that feature a real world brand name or logo should be modified to no longer feature said brand name, for example the box of doughnuts featured in **Act 2** was originally modified to read 'JimBits'. This separates the world of the play from the real world as all brands are different.

There should be a clear stylistic difference between any and all props belonging to **BadMan** compared to props belonging to any other character. For example, weapons such as **Alan's** or **Connor's** pistols should be realistic in both appearance and sound effects (**Alan's** pistol may have a more absurd sound, like that of a more powerful gun, as this adds to his characterisation as a stereotypical gun toting American.) whereas **BadMan's** weapon, **The Bad-Blaster** should look far less realistic and there should be no sound effect, instead **BadMan** should shout "Bang!" (A toy gun or water pistol could be used if any branding is removed and optionally replaced with a **Bad-Blaster** label.)

Large Cardboard signs should be worn by the performers, displaying each characters' name in thick black text. These signs showcase the absurdist tone to the audience, show when an actor is portraying a new character if a performance uses multi-roling, and add to the Brechtian style of the piece as they create an abnormal image that the audience will remember and allow the world the play is set in to remain distinct from the real world. This alienates the audience which is the goal of the Brechtian style. The signs also serve the secondary purpose of being the name-tags used by the crew in **Act 2** and worn by the guards in **Act 3.**

Due to the Brechtian style of the play, any amount of props could be mimed rather than physically made if this is more convenient for the individual performance. However, assuming every prop was made a complete prop list would consist of:

A boom mic for **Scott**.	Bad-Phone for **Scott**.
A flask for **Scott**.	Money for **The Director** to pick up.
A phone for **Scott**.	A pistol for **Connor**.
A camera for **Alan**.	Walkie Talkie for **Connor**.
A revolver for **Alan**.	Baton for **Ken**.
Bad-Blaster for **BadMan**.	Baton for **Donald**.
2 Burlap Sacks for **BadMan**.	Iron Brew Extra bottle for **Donald**.
Molotov cocktail for **BadMan**.	Doughnut (JimBits) box.
Rope for **BadMan**.	Dynamite box.
Bad-Phone for **BadMan**.	A cane for **Richard**.

(The camera gear **Alan** puts away on page 6 in Act 1 is part of the set and should be mimed but can be considered a prop.)

3-Characters:

BadMan – Full name; **Bad Evil Man. BadMan** is an unapologetic tribute to old cartoon villains such as Dick Dastardly, Snidely Whiplash, Skeletor and any other character that fit the 'moustache twirling villain' archetype. His goal is to rob a bank, he is so caught up in this goal that he has not yet considered what to do with the money he plans to steal. This character flaw is indicative of his personality, he lives for villainy, bad deeds are not a means to an end for him but instead a way of life. His characterisation reflects this. The **BadMan** Flavour of Evil is not that of a vicious monster but instead a vile fiend (Less terrorism and more taking a baby's pacifier and cackling at the mothers annoyance at the ensuing crying.) despite this he is not a joke and is still a threat as shown with his murdering of **Donald Dee.**

For an actor portraying **BadMan**, an ideal performance can be summarised with 'The three 'E's': *Eponymous-* **BadMan** is the title character and should act almost as if he knows this, soaking up every single second of stage time by being as strongly characterised as possible. **Eccentric- BadMan** is absurd even by an absurdist's standards. While the entire play is ridiculous and strange to the audience, **BadMan** is ridiculous and strange to his fellow characters, he should be over-the-top more often than not accompanied by a nefarious laugh. **Enigmatic- BadMan** and the inner workings of his mind should be a mystery to the characters and the audience. Where did he come from? Does he have Amnesia? Is his name actually **Bad E. Man**? How much of what he says to himself and others is true? Does it matter? The voice should be reminiscent of Skeletor but distinguished like Dick Dastardly.

BadMan's outfit should be simple, a somewhat distinguished outfit which is predominantly black with optional purple accents and a black bowler hat. For inspiration see Snidely Whiplash or Goob. **BadMan** does not necessarily need facial hair as he is of indeterminate age (He could be anywhere from twenty to sixty years old depending on the performance.) however providing him an evil goatee or a long thin moustache to twirl does aid the aesthetic. Aside from the hat, **BadMan** should have no form of facial covering, not only for more readable expressions in performance, but also as he doesn't want his crimes to be anonymous.

BadMan's behaviour by the time of his comeuppance should go from whimsical and childlike to irritated and snappy as he becomes tested by the people surrounding him (This parallels **The Director.**)

The Director – Full name; unneeded, **The Director** is completely in his own world and assumes that everybody is already familiar with his work and his life, as a result he never tells anyone his name assuming it to be common knowledge. Similarly, **The Director** never gets anyone else's name right, instead he confidently says any name assuming himself to be correct.

The defining trait of **The Director** for a performer to capture is his unique flavour of arrogance; he is completely absorbed in his own work and is arrogant not because he believes himself to be the best, but instead because he thinks the world sees his creations the same way he does. In this sense despite being more grounded than the rest of the characters, **The Director** is the most delusional as his films are all low budget B-Movies yet in his eyes he is a beloved artist and genius. A performer should also capture the passive aggressiveness of **The Director** as a result of him being surrounded by incompetence he should seem exacerbated with his situation with a facade of calmness that is deteriorated with every appearance until his breaking point in Act 2 before being restored for his happy ending in Act 3. He should seem like a loose canon, that the crew fear could go off at any moment, seemingly about to scream into a pillow before most lines. Many of his lines should be filled with fake chuckles and scoffs to obviously mask his panic and anger, he should also have a nasally yet nondescript American accent.

The Director should have a simple costume, a long, plain coat or jacket that he can quickly wave behind him, perhaps a beret or scarf or other similar additions to match the cocky film student trope, a simple shirt with a loosened tie and the top button undone, his appearance should become more dishevelled with each scene to show his stress building. This could be achieved by making his hair or clothes more messy with each appearance.

Scott – Full name; **Scott L. And. Scott** is a member of the film crew tasked with being the boom mic operator, however his defining traits are his alcoholism and his sheer Scottish-ness. Each of the three crew members are absurdist subversions of stereotypes of specific areas, with **Scott** being an alcoholic with a thick Scottish accent, the absurdism comes from Scottish tropes and the fact he has been in a perpetually drunken state for fifteen years. The subversion with **Scott** is that due to his impulsive decision to commit the entirety of the thesaurus to memory he becomes the most intelligent of the group with the frequent use of large words and eloquent sentences that do not match his demeanour in the slightest.

A performer should have a convincing Scottish accent and slurred speech, with stumbling physicality such as shaky steps to show drunkenness. The extent to which **Scott** knows what he is saying should also be left up to the audience. In terms of costume **Scott** should dress like a typical boozer, perhaps a Scottish football team shirt with a beer stain, he should always have a **flask** on him.

Scott also uses a lot of Scottish slang, a key of which is included:

Dinnae – Don't

Didnae – Didn't

Havenae – Haven't

Hasnae – Hasn't

Isnae – Isn't

Wasnae – Wasn't

Aye – Yes

Polis – Police

Alan – Full name; **Alan Bama. Alan** is the cameraman who is newer to the job than the other two crew members and as a result is more naïve. The defining trait of **Alan** is his American-ness. The absurdism with **Alan** comes from how patriotic he is, having the voice and mannerisms of an old western prospector. The subversion with **Alan** comes from the contrast between his old-timey characterisation and his young age and naïvety.

A performer portraying Alan should have a convincing southern accent with an old sheriff style of speaking. As **Alan** has fewer lines than **Richard** and **Scott** it is even more important for a performer portraying **Alan** to have comedic physicality, stance and facial expressions.

In terms of outfit, **Alan** could either dress like a sheriff or a stereotypical southern trucker with a **revolver** hidden in his vest until it is used.

Richard – Full name; **Richard Heddison. Richard** is another member of the crew. Nobody quite knows what his job is, not even himself. The defining trait of **Richard** is his sheer posh-ness. The absurdism of **Richard** comes from how prim and proper he behaves, to the point of over-pronouncing words, for example he pronounces **Alan** "Alaan". He also calls **BadMan** "Mr Man", and stresses the 'S' in **Scott.**

The subversion with **Richard** comes from the fact that despite his seemingly intelligent way of speaking most of what he says is either wrong or completely insubstantial, spoken in a way that attempts to seem profound. All of the characters see through **Richard** and do not actually believe him to be highly intelligent.

A performer portraying Richard must be able to capture his insane posh-ness, with constant posturing and stances that seem like he is posing for a marble statue as well as a posh English accent that has whiny undertones.

In terms of costume, he should be well dressed, with a shirt and tie, a cricket jumper, or other posh tweed clothes. He also carries a **cane** only for posing and making his walking seem even more posh. During the bank robbery it should be held out like a weapon wielded by someone who has never used a weapon before.

Ken – Full name; **Ken A. Dian.** Less a character and more of an extra, **Ken** is the first bank security guard and is a Canadian stereotype whose politeness is so absurd he apologises for being shot. He should speak with a thick rural Canadian accent and should be dressed in a guard uniform. He must have a moustache. His line deliveries and general movement should seem very timid and unsure. He should carry a **baton.**

Donald – Full name; **Donald Dee.** Another character that is more of an extra, **Donald** is the second bank security guard and is also Scottish. However, he is not an alcoholic and is instead a more distinguished Scotsman than **Scott.** He is still an absurd stereotype as his infatuation with **Iron Brew** is his downfall. He should also be dressed in a guard uniform. He should go from confident and imposing to weak and enamoured once **Iron Brew** is brought up. He should carry a **baton.**

Connor – Full name; **Connor Stable.** Another character that is more of an extra, **Connor** is the police officer who he is partly responsible for the downfall **BadMan** and is a tribute to the incompetent policeman trope. All of his deliveries should show that he has a cold, with frequent sniffing and a nasally, weak voice. He should be dressed in standard policeman attire and carry a **pistol.**

BadMan

a very bad play

Act 1

[Spotlight on **BadMan**]

BadMan (theatrically)

To bad?
Or not to Bad?
That is the question,
The bad question,
A bad question asked by only the baddest of bad men,
The baddest bad man.
I am BadMan.
And for as long as I can remember I have had but one bad dream,
Not a nightmare, but a wish,
A wish to rob a bank,
A bad bank.
I am lost.
Lost in a bad world,
A bad world for a bad man.
I am Bad E. Man.
And the E stands for Evil!

The Director Cut!

[Spotlight is removed as *The Stage* becomes fully lit revealing the set. **BadMan** is sat on the block with **Scott** beside him putting the boom mic down. **Richard** is at the desk, soon joined by **Scott. Alan** is Downstage left with the camera gear, **The Director** is behind him.]

The Director Terry, the hell was that?

(to Alan)

Alan Uh, boss? What's it look like? That there is our lead.

The Director He's awful. I hate him. **(turning to BadMan)** I hate you! What are you an idiot or something, do you need me to spell it out for you, I H-A-T-E you!

Richard Uhm, actually boss, there isn't an

(interjecting) 'I'or a 'U' in hate. **(scoffs poshly)**

[**The Director** pretends to not notice **Richard**, and inches closer to **Alan,** taking a step with each role listed.]

The Director Look Terry, I am already director, screenwriter, reserve actor, head of

	advertising, head of PR. I should not have to be a casting director as well.
Alan (pleading)	But boss! He's so committed!
Scott (pleading)	He hasnae even read the script yet and he's already in character!
Richard (pleading)	He even wrote his name as BadMan on the contract!
Scott	I think he has amnesia, reminds me of back home, when I hit me pal so hard I broke his skull, just 'cause of the football. I'm a good Scotsman like that.

[**Scott** takes a swig of his **flask** as the Scottish national anthem plays loudly. **Richard**, **Alan** and **The Director** each look around to see where the sound is coming from whereas **BadMan** sits still with his fingers tented as if he is plotting something.]

Scott	Sorry lads, that's me ringtone **(clicks phone, stopping the anthem)**
The Director	What makes you think he's got

	amnesia?
Richard	Well he wrote his name as BadMan on the contract.
The Director	You said that already.
Alan	But for everything else he just wrote question marks.
The Director	Wait, so you have no idea where he came from?
Alan	I wouldn't say "no idea" we know we found him on the street.
The Director (seemingly annoyed)	So you just grabbed him and handed him a contract, with no idea where he came from?
Richard	Well...
The Director (realising)	And no address to send pay-checks to?
Richard (confused)	I suppose so...
The Director (hastily)	You're hired! Just remember to read the script.

BadMan (feigning ignorance)	What script?
The Director	Alright everyone lets just take a quick break to get ready for the Martini Shot over at my apartment complex.

[BadMan leaves to go to *The Bad-Cave.*]

Scott	Martini Shot? You mean you've been doin' this sober?
The Director	You mean you haven't?
Scott	I havenae been sober for fifteen years pal! As a matter of fact it's me anniversary soon, you can come down to me house and 'ave a few pints.
The Director	As much as I would love to celebrate your anti-sobriety party, I have a million other things I would rather be doing.
Scott	Suit yourself, more booze for me.

[**Scott** swigs his **flask** and exits *Stage Right* while **Alan** puts away camera gear, visibly frustrated. **The Director** notices this and approaches him.]

The Director (patronizing)	Hey hey hey! Terry what's up with you?
Alan	Well boss its-
The Director (cutting in)	Ah ah ah, say no more Terry I understand completely.
Alan	Well that's good, since-
The Director (cutting in)	It's 'cause you're green.
Alan (agitated)	Excuse you! What part of this all American skin looks even a teensy bit green to you?
Richard	He isn't even wearing any green sir.
The Director (annoyed)	It means new Leonard!
Richard	My name is Richard.
Alan	That's my problem right there.
The Director	What? The crew? I can understand that, you see on the set of my first

movie; 'Shark-Tornado XVII; Return of The Attack of The Killer Orca Typhoon'-

Alan (annoyed) No dang nabbit not the crew! You getting' my name wrong is the problem here. My name ain't Terry it's Alan Bama, Al for short.

The Director (dismissively) Okay Tear Bear.

Alan Oh come on!

[**Alan** exits *Stage Left.*]

The Director (unbothered) Leonard! Get the sparklers from the back we'll need them for the explosion effects at my apartment complex.

Richard But sir, I'm not in charge of the effects.

The Director Then what are you in charge of?

Richard (unconfident) Well... um... I suppose...

The Director Go get the sparklers Leonard.

(bluntly)

Richard Yes sir.

(defeated)

[**Richard** exits *Stage Right.*]

The Director God this is a mess.

(exasperated)

[**The Director** exits *Stage Left* as the lights go out on the stage and *The Bad-Cave* becomes lit up with **BadMan** at the flipboard, displaying a bad drawing of a bank.]

BadMan God this is perfect! Those imbecilic

(elated) ignoramuses don't suspect a thing, no concerns about who I am, no monitoring of my actions, nothing! This place will make the perfect cover for my bank robbery, I mean I can announce my plans aloud in full detail and they'll just think I'm acting. Oh pretending to have amnesia **(cackle)** that's the oldest trick in the book.

[**The Director** enters *Stage Left* and begins to slowly creep down the steps and towards **BadMan.**]

BadMan — Now back to the plan. If there is a guard here and here **(drawing two 'X's on top of the drawing of the bank)** then it looks like I'll have to tune up the patented Bad-Blaster.

[**BadMan** takes out the **Bad-Blaster** and aims for the 'X's on the flipboard, with each shot he fires he gets pushed back, causing **The Director** to take a step back as well.]

BadMan **(firing)** — Bang! Bang! Bang! It's no good, if I can't get this working I'll never be able to achieve my dream of robbing a bank! **(cackle)** And if I can't do that then I'll never be able to... to... Come to think of it I've wanted to rob a bank for so long, and yet I never stopped to consider what I would do with the money. **(with a devious grin)**

Maybe I should farm something... like leaves... Yes Bad.E.Man – leaf farmer that sounds good.

[**The Director** has crept up behind **BadMan** and gives a slow clap.]

The Director (in disbelief) — Wow. Just... wow.

BadMan — **(high pitched scream)**

[**BadMan** and **The Director** each freeze for a moment, unsure of what they just heard.]

The Director (in awe) — You can act girl roles as well!

BadMan — What do you mean "act girl roles"?

The Director (casually) — Oh come on, you don't have to lie to me.

BadMan (concerned) — Uhhh...

[**BadMan** readies the **Bad-Blaster** slyly behind his back.]

The Director (assuredly) — I mean, it's obvious you don't have amnesia.

[**BadMan** turns away from **The Director.**]

BadMan (whispering loudly) Drats! Perhaps these dunderheads aren't as foolish as I thought.

The Director You're a method actor.

BadMan (muttering) Just roll with it BadMan.

[**BadMan** quickly lowers the **Bad-Blaster** and swings back around to face **The Director.**]

BadMan (putting on a facade) Oh darn! You caught me red handed boss.

The Director Well I am quite perceptive.

BadMan (muttering) About as perceptive as a blind man at night.

The Director What was that?

BadMan Nothing.

The Director Well I was only here because I was looking for the sparklers, I swear Rupert is so difficult, I mean they're right here.

[**The Director** grabs the **dynamite box** from behind the flipboard.]

The Director (reading slowly) Dynamite...

BadMan I wouldn't...

The Director It's a different brand than usual but if my lead is going to buy his own pyrotechnics I wont complain.

BadMan (fake) I wouldn't do anything less boss **(fake laugh).**

The Director (passive aggressivity) You know, I was wrong about you. I mean I know I'm very subtle but I did *not* like you. Between your stupid face, your stupid shoes, your complete disregard for my script, your awful voice, your stupid face, your horrible work ethic and of course your stupid face I was ready to throw you back on the streets and keep your hat as a reminder for the rest of the crew, but now I can see that I was wrong, you are-

[**BadMan** begins sobbing in an exaggerated fashion.]

The Director (unsure) Crying? Oh my God you're actually crying... ah... well I... Um. Your break is over so we'll be waiting in the car. You just pull yourself together.

[**The Director** goes back up the *Stage Left Steps* and exits *Stage Left* as **BadMan's** sobbing transitions into maniacal laughter.]

BadMan (through mad laughter) Ha! Ha! Ha! Be right there boss! Oh thank goodness he's such a fool. I could tell him about the dynamite... but I'd rather see where this goes.

[**BadMan** goes up the steps and exits *Stage Left* all the while still laughing maniacally. Curtains close as if to go to intermission, there is no intermission, the beginning of Act 2 plays behind the curtains.]

Act 2

The Director	Alright, final shot of the day. Brendan! Is the camera set up?
Alan	I think so.
The Director	Fergus! Did you remember to turn the mic on?
Scott	Aye.
The Director	Oliver! Did you set up the sparklers?
Richard	Yes sir, but I couldn't help but notice that something was wrong with them.
BadMan (drawn out)	No...
The Director	What was wrong with them?
Richard	Well they weren't sparkling.
BadMan	Phew.
The Director (let down)	I think we'll be fine. Three, two, one act-

[A phone rings]

The Director	Actually I'll have to take this, the

producers are calling about the budget, you guys will have to take care of this last shot.

[Loud fiery explosion plays followed by mic ringing. The sounds abruptedly end as the curtains pull back to reveal the set with **Alan, Richard** and **Scott** sat at the desk with the **doughnut box.** The three of them are applying name tags to themselves.]

Richard Are you sure these things will work?

Scott They have to, I mean we've literally spelt it out for him.

The Director (offstage) Jonas!

Alan Or not.

[**The Director** enters *Upstage Left* and storms towards the desk.]

The Director Jonas! Where's my money?

Richard (half smug) Have you checked your pockets sir? **(posh scoff).**

The Director (forcing out) **(fake laugh)** Very funny, *Maurice*! I mean the budget money. The

producers and I *finally* agreed
on a budget after last night's call
but when I called this morning to ask
when I would get the money, they told
me they already sent the money here.
In cash. So where is it?

[**Alan, Richard** and **Scott** each look towards the **doughnut box** in unison.]

Scott Ugh...
(drawn out)
(in unison)
Alan Ugh...
(drawn out)
(in unison)
Richard Ugh...
(drawn out)
The Director You didn't?
Richard Yes.
Alan Uh-huh.
Scott Aye.

The Director Eleven *million* dollars!
(confounded)

[**The Director** is standing at the table seething with rage as **Alan** pushes the doughnut box over to him.]

The Director No I don't want any!
(outraged)

[**The Director** slaps the **doughnut box** off of the table revealing it to be empty.]

The Director You guys spent... *eleven million*
(shakily) *dollars...* on doughnuts and didn't
even save any for me!

Alan I just wanted you to put it in the
(meekly) trash can boss.

Richard In all fairness you didn't really ask
(muttering for any sir.
meekly)

The Director Maurice! Eleven million dollars!
(exploding) That is a *lot* of money! I had to pull
so many strings to get all that cash...

(miming weaving a rope) so many strings I could weave them together into a nice tight rope and hang myself with it... and I really want to hang myself right now... **(with a facade of composure)** but, we've got a film to make, we've got scenes to shoot, and I have footage to edit. So I am going to go into my office, and I am going to look over the footage from last night's shoot.

Scott (whispering) Hang on does he not know about-

Richard (whispering) I suppose not.

Alan Uh sir-

[**The Director** storms off and exits *Upstage Left.*]

Scott Speakin' of last night's shoot, did anything seem a bit... off about BadMan to you lot?

Richard — Well now that you mention it, he did seem a quite weird.

Alan — Howdya mean?

Richard — He just seems to be a little bit... un-truthtelling.

Alan — Now that ain't a word limey.

Scott — Yeah pal, I think you might mean deceptive, or treacherous, or maybe even duplicitous.

Alan — Woah what's with all the big words there Scott?

Scott — I got hammered last night and accidentally read the whole thesaurus.

Richard (smugly) — "Got hammered"? Wouldn't that mean you weren't before?

Scott — (producing air quotes) "Got hammered". "Was hammered". There isnae any need for pedantry.

Richard — I am not a peasant!

Scott — Shut up! We were talkin' about somethin' weren't we?

Alan — Yeah. Y'all were talking about BadMan.

Richard — Oh yes! I believe he may be faking his amnesia.

Alan — Really?

Scott — It would make sense. The pal I gave amnesia wasnae exactly bangin' on about his "master plan" or his "incredible deception". Then again he wasnae exactly bangin' about anything seein' as I broke his skull.

[**The Director** enters *Upstage Left* standing still, frozen by infuriation, going unnoticed.]

Alan — Actually come to think of it, I guess you could be right. BadMan is pretty weird, like earlier today I overheard him in the green room, he kept calling it his "Bad-Cave".

Richard	Well that is a better name, than "green room", I mean it wasn't even green.
Alan	Stupid Limey. The green room is just the lounge for the actors and crew, not just a room that's green.
Richard	Well why is it not green?
Alan	That's just what their called, the earliest ones were green but people don't fully know where the term comes from.
Richard	How on earth do you know that?
Alan	D'yall remember yesterday when the boss got mad that I didn't know green meant new?
Scott	Aye.
Alan	Well during the break he gave me this here book filled with film set terms and told me to memorise it. He even said if I played my cards right I

could take over for him.

Richard	Playing cards? I thought poker night was tomorrow.
Scott (dismissive)	It is, he means if anything bad happens to the boss then he can take over for him... Hang on I just had a thought, if we're right and there is something off about BadMan, then what if those 'Dynamite Sticks' were more than just a faulty sparkler brand...
Alan (realising)	What if they were actual dynamite sticks!
Richard	You mean to say that what happened last night was his idea... that it was on purpose?
Scott (noticing)	This might have to wait ... I think the boss has seen the footage.
The Director (powerfully)	Ahem!

[**Scott, Alan** and **Richard** each slowly pivot in unison while standing up straight, petrified expressions on their faces, stopping once facing **The Director,** who is poorly masking rage behind a facade of composure.]

The Director (robotically)	Ferris.
Richard (whispering)	**(leaning in to Alan)** I think you might be Ferris.
Alan (shakily)	Yeah boss?
The Director	So I was just checking the dailies-
Richard (shakily)	W-what were you checking every day sir? **(forced chuckle)**
The Director	**(sharp inhale followed by forced sigh)** Ferris, could you please?
Alan (entranced)	Yes boss. **(clears throat)** Dailies are the unedited footage for a movie or TV show that is collected at the end of each day for viewing by select above-the-line members of the film

	crew. Hey I guess that book did help.
The Director	Great, thanks, now I was just checking *the dailies* and noticed something really weird about last night's shoot.
Alan	Well uh...
The Director (breaking)	If you look at it right you can kinda notice...that all the footage is black. Almost as if some overpaid camera-man left the cap on the camera, and for some reason the audio just cuts out.
Alan (relieved)	Phew, well sir-
The Director	Not to mention the fiery explosion.
Alan	Darn it! Look boss we can explain. The explosion was Bad-
The Director	Woah, woah, woah. My problem isn't with the explosion.
Alan	Really?

The Director Really. I can sleep in a scrapyard if I have to, hell it's where I slept last night. My problem is that the biggest practical effect in the history of my career *wasn't caught on camera!*

Richard (cautiously) So you aren't angry that we blew up a building?

The Director No...

Richard Well that's good-

The Director (bluntly) I'm furious.

Alan But you said-

The Director (ticked off) I'm fine losing a random building, but you blew up my apartment complex Ferris, and all the footage is gone.

Richard Well can't they just rebuild it?

The Director (exploding) Oh they're gonna rebuild it! But can you guess who has to pay for it?

Richard You sir?

The Director (furious)	Ding! Ding! Ding! Yes it's me! And it's going to cost me another *eleven! Million! Dollars!* I am now twenty two million dollars in debt!
Richard	Um actually boss the two eleven million dollars cancel each other out.
Alan	Y'hear that boss? You ain't in debt no more.
The Director (accusingly)	Shut up! **(sharp inhale)** Peter, what happened to all the audio?
Richard (whispering)	**(leaning in to Scott)** I think you might be Peter.
Scott (insincere)	Ya think?
The Director	Ahem.
Scott	Well...
The Director	Well?
Scott (unbothered)	Well you see, the building went boom...

The Director (realising)	No...
Scott	And it's called a boom mic...
The Director (urgently)	No no no.
Scott	So I put the boom in the boom.
Alan	Oh I get it. **(chuckles)**
Richard (through laughter)	You see sir, it's funny because-
The Director (erupting)	I see the Irony Eugene! That's it...I'm done. I am sick of all of you. You are all, by far the least professional, most atrocious excuses for employees I have ever had the displeasure of working with! And I have had to work with sharks! I will see all of you in Hell!

[**The Director** storms off enraged, exiting *Upstage Left.*]

Scott (whispering) — **(leaning in to Richard)** I think you might be Eugene.

[Brief pause.]

Alan — He... he'll be back... right?

Richard — Of course he will.

Scott — Aye pall, he's just blowing off some steam, I'm sure he'll be back in a minute.

[The light moves down to to **BadMan** in *The Bad-Cave*. The flipboard now displays a childish drawing of a police officer.]

BadMan — **(maniacal laughter)** Several weeks have passed since that dunderhead director left and now my master plan is nearing completion and everything is going swimmingly if I do say so myself.

[**Alan** enters coming down the *Stage Left Steps* moving behind **BadMan.**]

Alan — Okay BadMan you're break is up-

BadMan — **(high pitched scream)**

[Brief pause.]

Alan (taken aback) — Your break is up, so we need you on set in ten to shoot your big cop scene and probably the car chase too.

BadMan (muttering) — Shoot the cops... Alan! You've read my mind!

[**BadMan** takes out the **Bad-Blaster** shooting the flipboard, shouting "Bang!" with each shot fired. Once he has finished **Richard** appears atop of the *Stage Left Steps*.]

Richard — Alaan?

BadMan — (high pitched scream)

[Brief pause.]

Richard (taken aback) — (walking down the *Stage Left Steps*) Oh yes. Alaan, you're needed on the camera if you don't mind.

[**Scott** enters from the top of *Stage Left Steps* in a more drunk fashion than normal. **The curtains close so that the stage can be set for Act 3.**]

Scott — Oi ya English scum-

BadMan — (high pitched scream)

[**Scott** drunkenly descends the *Stage Left Steps* as **BadMan** returns to his plotting.]

Scott (unfazed) — Where's the booze!?

Alan — C'mon now Scott don't you know the hooch on film sets is just water and food dye?

Scott — C-Course I knew that... It's just that I finished me stash and I need me fix.

Richard — Deary, deary me. I'd imagine the boss kept some in his office, after all he certainly began to go off the "deep end" as it were.

Alan — Speakin' off the man, where in tarnation is he?

Scott — Havenae a clue, last time I'd seen him was when he stormed out.

Richard (vaguely concerned) — But that was some time ago now, I mean I know Alaan has been taking over directing but he can't do that forever, we'll need him back at some point.

Alan (snapping) I don't care about the useless piece of crud, if you ask me his messin's been going on for too long, even if he does come back, I might just quit!

Richard (perturbed) Why Alaan that's a preposterous idea! How could you abandon our dear friend- Um... Our dear friend... Oh wow he never did tell us his name, did he?

Scott Aye, an' he never got our names right either! You know what I'm with Alan, I say we terminate our contracts.

Richard (shocked) Terminate!? We aren't going to kill him Scott!

Scott **(groan)** Well BadMan what d'ya say?

Alan Yeah BadMan-

[**Alan** turns to **BadMan**, who has prepared for the robbery with the **Bad-Blaster** ready and two empty **burlap sacks.**]

Alan (shocked) What the cheesin' cussin' Chris are you up to?

BadMan (alarmed) You're still here?

Alan Well where else would we be?

BadMan (flimsily) **(to himself)** Improvise BadMan... Um I'm just getting ready for the bank robbery *we've* been planning this whole time... right.

Scott (annoyed) Oh would ya just stop already, we all know you're lyin'. You don't really have amnesia, it's all just a big farce.

Alan Yeah so just fess up!

BadMan (clearly lying) **(to himself)**...Eureka! **(slowly clapping)** Well, well, well looks like you've caught me out, well if the cat's out of the bag I guess I have no choice-

Richard (shocked) You were keeping a cat in that bag?

BadMan	**(sighing)** I guess I have no choice but to tell you all the truth.
Richard	Well it's about time Mr Man.
BadMan (theatrically)	For you see, I am more than just a mere amnesiac, as you're bumbling boss figured out, however I am not just some "method actor" either, a fact your boss never had the chance to uncover-
Richard (interjecting)	**(posh gasp)** You killed him!
BadMan	No, you posh putz, he just quit before he learnt the real truth. I plan to rob a bank! **(evil laugh)**
Alan	Yeah we know, it's in the script.
BadMan (theatrically)	No, not for your movie, for real. The Bank Down-Town has a vault with twenty-three million dollars in cold hard cash, and now I'm finally ready to rob it! However, as you have all

caught me in my devious rouse I suppose I shall let you accompany me, for an even split of the goods of course.

Alan (unsure) Well uhm...

Scott (stalling) Y'see pal...

Richard (stammering) I suppose...

BadMan (dramatic) Perfect! To The Bad-Mobile!

[**BadMan** whimsically skips to *The Bad-Mobile* jumping into the driver's seat like an excitable child, **Alan, Scott**, and **Richard** follow less enthused.]

Richard So your whole plan was to use our movie as a cover to plan your bank robbery. Were you even going to tell us?

BadMan (lying) **(steering)** Of course I was going to tell you all, I was simply waiting for the perfect moment, where you have nothing left to lose.

Scott — I could lose me drinking arm.

BadMan — But after this you could have all the booze in the world! And I'll finally be able to achieve my dream of robbing a bank!

Scott — S'ppose so. **(takes a massive swig)**

BadMan — **(stops steering)** Now, Scott how drunk are you?

Scott (drunkenly) — Aye.

BadMan — Perfect. Here take this Bad-Phone, you're the lookout. We're channel 2.

[**BadMan** hands **Scott The Bad-Phone.**]

Scott — Isnae this just a walkie talkie?

Richard (cowardly) — M-M-Mr man can't I be the lookout?

Scott — You better lookout unless ya wanna fight ya posh-

[**BadMan** honks the horn censoring **Scott's** cursing which is mouthed exaggeratedly.]

BadMan That's enough! We can't delay any longer.

Alan Then what are we waiting for? Let's bring home the bacon!

Richard This is a bank not a butchers.

[**BadMan, Alan** and **Richard** exit *The Bad-Mobile* and creep towards the *Stage Right Steps* which they ascend as the curtains pull back.]

BadMan (creeping) **(progressively louder)** Alan! Be quiet! Be quiet! Alan! You have to be quiet!

[**Alan** remains completely silent.]

Act 3

[*Stage Right* becomes lit while *Stage Left* stays dark, a desk is visible with a laptop atop it, **BadMan**, **Alan** and **Richard** are huddled together in a conspicuous manner **Ken** is standing *Centre Stage* in a timid attempt at a guardsman stance.]

BadMan (loudly whispering)	Alright, so here's what we'll do, I'll get to deactivating the lasers on this computer.

[**BadMan** crouches at the laptop and starts 'Hollywood hacking' tapping random keys quickly.]

BadMan	Now Alan, you'll need to-
Ken (apologetic)	Sorry to interrupt your bank robbery but I might just have to ask you to stop right there it's aboot time you come with me, now.
BadMan	**(through gritted teeth)** -Get him.
Richard (flustered)	But Mr Man! You haven't given us any weapons!
Alan	Right on boss! **(pulling out a gun)**
Richard	Alaan! Where did you get that!

[**BadMan** keeps hacking, **Richard** seems visibly panicked, holding his **cane** out shakily as some form of a weapon. **Alan** poses like a cowboy in a stand-off as the American National Anthem plays.]

Alan (exuding patriotism)	Second Amendment limey, right to keep and bear arms. **(kisses revolver)** That ain't even my ringtone, that just happens when I bring up the constitution.

[The American national anthem stops playing.]

Richard (urgently)	Yes Alaan I know you have arms! I'm talking about the *gun!* Where did you get the gu-
Alan	Freedom!

[**Alan** shoots **Ken** who falls to the ground.]

Ken (weakly)	Oh sorey for getting in the way of yer bullet there, go fill yer boots, eh, sorey for causing a kerfuffle there...
Alan	Roll Tide. **(blows smoke from pistol and spins it)**
Richard	My goodness Alaan you shot Scott!

Alan	That ain't Scott ya knucklehead, this feller's got a moustache.
Richard	But he looks just like him.
Alan	And yet he's got himself a moustache.
Richard	Could he have been Scott's brother?
Alan	**(leaning over Ken)** Nope. Says here his name is Ken. 'Ken A. Dian'.
Richard (racking his brain)	Oh, well then he can't be Scott, for you see Scott's last name is And... something and his middle name... oh this is going to bother me for while, um. Well I know it starts with an 'L'.

[**BadMan** finishes hacking and gets up holding his **Bad-Blaster** close to his chest.]

BadMan	Enough pun names, I've deactivated the lasers, let's go!

[*Stage Right* becomes dark while *Stage Left* becomes lit, revealing a large safe. **Donald** is standing near the *Left Wing* in a more confident stance than **Ken** had, **baton** in hand.]

BadMan	There's the safe boys!

[**BadMan** takes a comically large, slow step forward. As his foot finally meets the ground, **Donald** walks forward.]

Donald (powerfully) Oi!

BadMan **(high pitched scream)**

[**BadMan** sharply jumps backwards ending up in a huddle with **Alan** and **Richard.**]

Donald (imposing) What are you lot doin' here, and what did you do to old Kenny?

Richard (blurting out) We killed him because we're here to rob this bank!

[**Richard** is wincing as **Alan** readies his **revolver** nonchalantly. **BadMan** readies the **Bad-Blaster**, unclear **if** it's to shoot **Donald** or **Richard.**]

Donald (confidently) Well we cannae be havin' that. You lot are comin' with me, or my name isnae Donald Dee.

Richard **(to himself)** Cannae? Isnae? **(posh gasp)** Guns down everyone I believe this guardsman may be Scottish, and

I've happened to have learnt some Scottish from Scott.

[**BadMan** and **Alan** reluctantly comply as **Donald** raises his **baton** to strike them.]

Richard (mustering up courage) By Jove, would you look at that, some Iron Brew!

[**Donald** stops his baton strike at the last possible moment and turns to **Richard** like an excited child on Christmas morning.]

Donald (disbelief) Iron Brew? Where?

Richard (theatrically) Well right over there inside that safe.

[**Donald** turns swiftly and dashes to the safe with the same desperation as a starving man promised food, as soon as his back is turned **BadMan** readies his **Bad-Blaster** and aims.]

Donald (entranced) **(reciting with each step)** Iron Brew. Original recipe. 1901.

[**Donald** opens the safe, going from manic to depressed in an instant.]

Donald (devastated) Oh no. It's just Iron Brew Extra... and millions o' dollars in cold hard cash.

BadMan Perfect. Bang!

[**BadMan** shoots **Donald** who falls to the floor, still holding the bottle.]

Donald (dejected) Oh, kick a man while he's down why don't ya!

BadMan (smugly) If you say so.

[**BadMan** kicks him down enthusiastically clearly having a blast and continues as lights move from *The Stage* to *The Bad-Mobile* as Scott sits holding up **The Bad**-Phone, racking his brain.]

Scott They sure are taking a while, what if somethin's gone awry. I better call them, but which channel was it? I think he said channel 3.

[**Scott** tunes **The Bad-Phone** and holds it closer.]

Scott (clearly) Oi, BadMan what's takin' ya so long, shouldn't you, *'Bad Evil Man'* as well as *'Richard Heddison'* and *'Alan*

Bama' be done with your robbery of the Bank Down Town by now? Hang on is that the sound of doughnuts bein' eaten... **(realising)** Oh No!

[**Scott** hastily hangs up **The Bad-Phone** and tunes it to another channel.]

Scott (frantically) Channel 2. Channel 2. Channel 2.

[*The Stage* becomes fully lit revealing **BadMan** still kicking **Donald** almost dancing as **Richard** and **Alan** stand holding the full **burlap sacks.** *The Bad-Mobile* stays lit with **Scott** clenching **The Bad-Phone.**]

Richard Mr Man I believe he's dead by now.

BadMan I suppose. Oh The Bad-Phone is ringing, **(picking it up)** yellow.

Scott **(taking a deep calming breath, then exploding with urgency)** Hurry BadMan! The Polis are coming!

BadMan The Polish! After my last run-in with them I'm sure the police won't be too far behind them. This doesn't bode well. How did they catch on to us Scott?

Scott (sharply) Havenae a clue.

BadMan Alright new plan. Alan, take a bag and run all the way to the Bad-Mobile.

Alan On the double sir!

[**Alan** walks across *Stage Right.*]

BadMan Not the way we came you bumbling bumpkin! Find another way.

Alan (muttering) Okay I'll mosey on down this way then.

[**Alan** exits *Downstage Left* as **Richard** throws his **burlap sack** on the ground.]

Richard (finding backbone) Mr Man I must object, I shan't be an accomplice, alibi, or an accessory to your alliteration- I mean crime.

BadMan That's fine.

Richard Really sir?

BadMan	Of course, if you won't be helper you can always be a hostage.

[Generic Dun Dun Dun sting plays as **BadMan** aims **The Bad-Blaster** at **Richard.**]

Scott	Sorry BadMan, that's my new ringtone... Hang on what's this about a hostage?
BadMan (muttering)	This thing is still on?

[**Richard** inches away as **BadMan** and **Scott** keep their **Bad-Phones** to their faces.]

Scott	Hello? Did ya say somethin'.
BadMan	Nothing! Just press the Kidnapping Button on The Bad-Mobile control deck.
Scott	Why is my seat reclining?
BadMan	No not the Kid's Napping Button-
Scott	BadMan I must say I dinnae really like the implications of this button- Oh is that booze?
BadMan	Don't drink that!

Scott — Aw why not... Is that rope, BadMan the more I learn about your vehicle the less I know. I don't quite like the conclusions one could come to based off of what's presented here.

BadMan (dismissive) — Just grab the rope, the vodka, and hit the ejector seat button.

Scott — If it gets me out of this car quicker then sure thing.

[**Scott** grabs the **rope** and **vodka** and walks up the *Stage Left Steps* as if in an ejector seat, he lands on the floor sitting down.]

BadMan — You too Richard.

[**BadMan** grabs **Richard** and pushes him onto the floor next to **Scott** as **Alan** enters *Downstage Left*.]

Alan — Hey partner I couldn't find no other ex-

[**Alan** drops his **burlap sack** as **BadMan** points to **Scott** and **Richard**, **Alan** walks timidly and sits next to them.]

BadMan — Perfect.

[**BadMan** ties the three together and kicks both **burlap sacks** next to his own feet.]

BadMan (triumphant)	Now, in an ideal world where everything goes according to plan the dynamite means none of you will be hurt!
Richard (interjecting)	But you used all of your dynamite on the apartment complex.

[**BadMan** takes a second to think.]

BadMan (identically)	Some of you will get hurt!
Alan	I don't get it, why can't you just take the cash and turn tail?
BadMan	Because if I did the police would be on my back forever, a life on the run is not what I signed up for-
Scott	Well BadMan, as a bank robber, isnae evading the polis exactly what you signed up for?
BadMan	No, because great bank robbers such

as myself understand that they need to cover their tracks, so I will have to fake my death if I'm going to live out my days as a leaf farmer.

[**Richard**, **Scott** and **Alan** sit, dumbfounded.]

Alan (confused) Excuse you?

Scott (annoyed) Are you serious pal?

Richard (cautiously) At the risk of seeming rude Mr Man, you hardly need twenty-three million dollars for that, you know...

Scott (outraged) Seein' as they literally grow on trees!

Alan (naively) Let's not be too hasty now, he wouldn't have had twenty-three million bones, once we split it up he woulda had... five million, seven hundred and fifty thousand.

BadMan Putting aside my own amazement

that you can even do mathematics, you'd still be wrong. I was never going to split the money!

Alan (blown away)
Excuse you!

Scott (horrified)
You mean to tell me I jeopardized my drinking arm for a lie?

BadMan (breaking)
Yes you dipsomaniacal dim-wit! Are you really surprised I lied... Again?

Richard (justifying)
Well...

BadMan (dryly)
I literally said 'Eureka' and slow clapped.

Alan (sulking)
Well if we weren't getting the money, why bring us at all?

BadMan
When you all caught me out in my sham I seized the opportunity to use you fools as my fall guys. You give me a helping hand and then I

leave you all to die once you've served your purpose.

[Police sirens sound off as **Connor** enters at the bottom of the *Stage Right Steps*, he aims his gun at **BadMan** above him.]

Connor (sniffling) Alright, come down with your hands up and nobody has to get hurt.

BadMan (triumphant) And that's my cue to blow this joint, any last words before my explosive finale?

Scott (cautiously) Well BadMan, I suppose this is my only chance to ask... What was the deal with the Kid's Napping Button in the Bad-Mobile, 'cause I must say, I did not like where me mind went with that.

BadMan (offended) What, the Kid's Napping Button is just for stealing candy from babies. What else would it be for?

Scott **(exhaling)** Oh thank god.

Richard That's evil. Awful. Despicable!

BadMan	Bingo.
Alan	Hang on Richard, he is literally about to blow us up to kingdom come and that's your problem?
Richard (accusingly)	No Alaan, my problem is this... what is Mr Man's real name!
BadMan (quickly)	BadMan.
Richard	What?
BadMan (quickly)	BadMan.
Scott	No not your cover name, your real name.
BadMan	It's BadMan.
Richard (confused)	So hang on. You, BadMan, decided to stay under cover, in a film, called BadMan, as a method actor playing a character named BadMan, and there isn't any relation. That is quite the coincidence.

Alan	Yeah, really convenient for your bank robbery.
BadMan (defensive)	No! There's nothing convenient about this, this bank robbery is only going well because of my meticulous planning!
Scott	Not to rain on your parade BadMan but given the fact that all parties involved ended up seein' through your lies, was your planning really all that meticulous?
BadMan (irked)	Of course it was!
Alan	Not to stomp on your dreams mister, just a though, if you already had a gun then why didn't you just hold up the bank instead of messin' around with all this stealth nonsense.
Richard	Or you could've stolen the budget money, before we bought all of those

	doughnuts it was just lying by the door in a bag, surely that would have been more than sufficient.
BadMan (nettled)	Because I don't just steal for the money, I don't want to be handed my destiny, I shall seize it from the claws of the future and drag it to the present. I steal for the art.
Scott	That's oddly profound... but why not wear a mask at least.
BadMan (getting more annoyed)	Because I want the world to know who robbed this bank. Who they'll never catch. I will never hide my face, I'll keep this hat on my head and keep it high.
Richard	Well, not to spoil your day in the sun but it seems to me like you have purposefully made this more difficult for yourself.
Alan	Not to rustle your jimmies now, but

given the fact that this is your childhood dream, you'd think ya'd make your plan slightly more... airtight.

BadMan (reaching breaking point) Airtight!

Scott And not to grind your gears or anythin' but to have your whole plan revolve around breakin' into a bank, only to end up killin' the guards and blowin' the place up, kind of makes the planning a bit of a moot point. Right?

BadMan No Because-

Richard And not to ruffle your feathers, but would it not have been easier to rob the bank on a bank holiday Monday, after all, the guards would be on

	holiday.
Alan	We call 'em federal holidays limey.
BadMan	That would be stupid, because...
Alan	Now if you really wanted to burst his bubble, you'd point out that he coulda waited 'til the movie was done, ensure it made a truckload of cash, and then steal that so he'd still get the thrill, more money, and a more memorable story.
Scott	Aye you've got a point pal, bank robbery is a tad... generic.
BadMan (furious)	Generic!
Connor	Not to poop on your party, but I'm still here, so come down... now.
BadMan (snapping)	No! No! No! I've had enough of this, stop "blanking my blank" and leave me be!
Connor	I'm just doing what I'm supposed to.

BadMan (defiantly) — And so am I!

[**BadMan** and **Connor** continue a mouthed argument as the lights dim slightly, with a spotlight on **Alan**, **Scott** and **Richard.**]

Richard (whispering) — He seems rather fixated on this argument, this may be our chance to escape.

Alan — But we're still tied up...

Connor (negotiating) — Just put the C4 down and come out here with your hands up.

BadMan (insulted) — C4! What do I look like, some rank amateur! I'm burning this place down with a Molotov cocktail, thank you very much.

[**BadMan** and **Connor** continue their mouthed argument.]

Scott (distraught) — Oh God, I can't believe I'm gonna die to a cocktail. Oh the irony!

[**Scott** lets out an exaggerated sob, placing his hand onto his face revealing that he isn't tied up.]

Richard (suprised)	Great Scott!
Scott (sobbing)	Thanks, I am pretty great, or I guess it's 'was pretty great' now.
Richard	No I mean, look at you, you aren't tied up. How?
Scott	Aye, that's just a trick I picked up from my friend who dinnae.
Richard	What did he not do?
Scott	No pal, I think that was his surname.
Richard	Well it doesn't matter, if you're untied then it means you can get us out of here.
Alan	That doesn't matter, what we need to do is take BadMan out. Scott take my gun and shoot him before he notices.
Scott	Alright.

[**Scott** takes **Alan's pistol** and sneaks up behind **BadMan** as he aims **BadMan** turns.]

BadMan	Bang!

[**BadMan** fires the **Bad-Blaster** at **Scott** who falls to the ground clenching his shoulder, **Richard** and **Alan** wince as if they are about to be shot.]

Richard (shocked)	Scott no!
Alan (in disbelief)	Get up, partner!
BadMan (maniacal)	Seriously... Seriously! What did you think was going to happen, I warned you, you were warned, this is my moment, no more interruptions, no more witty remarks, just me and my moment!
Scott (weakly)	Dinnae worry laddies, I think we can all learn a lesson from this. How far should we go to achieve our dreams? Is it alright to harm others for the sake of our individuality? At what point should we give up on what we want, so that others can get what

	they need?
Richard (poetically)	And where do we even draw the line between needs and wants? When do we tell people that enough is enough? Is it even possible for everyone to get what they want in life?
Alan (assuredly)	Should we even encourage people to achieve their dreams? What if one person's dream clashes with someone else's?
Scott (wisdomous)	Is it okay to let people be bad just 'cause that's how they are?
Richard (wisely)	How bad is too bad?
Alan (poignantly)	If we do get everything we ever wanted, will it even satisfy us?
Scott	And-
BadMan (enraged)	Shut Up! I have had enough of this mind-numbing, brain-rotting,

	pseudo-intellectual drivel, this asinine yapping, this incessant irrelevant... garbage!
Richard	Well-
BadMan	No!
Alan	But-
BadMan	No!
Scott	Well-
BadMan (exploding)	No! No! No! I'm done playing around. I am sick of all of you. You are all, by far, the least professional, most atrocious excuses for cohorts, fall guys, or hostages I have ever had the displeasure of working with. I will see all of you in Hell!
Alan (recalling)	That sounds familiar.
Scott	I guess when we see ourselves as above others we become blind to how similar we are to one another.

BadMan (theatrically) Shut up! Stop trying to steal my moment! Stealing is my thing, and if you've got a problem with that,
Then that's too bad,
Or not too bad,
That is the question,
The bad question.
A bad question I've had since I was but a lad.
A bad lad.
A bad lad staring at the stars in the sky,
Wishing at every turn to make other's property mine.
I wanted to steal the sun and its shine.
I would steal dollars, nickels, quarters and dimes.
I took jewellery from mothers, and candy from infants,

Hide my tomfoolery from others, and disband in an instant.
A machine spitting lies, falsehoods in deceit,
With a keen stealing eye, took the receipts.
And I'll admit at times my lies were quite lazy,
But it wasn't all wrong to say that my memory's hazy,
Not from trauma, amnesia, nor a hit to the head,
But because I always looked on to the future instead.
For I steal for the thrill, the art and the passion,
And I always depart in a most memorable fashion. **(readying the Molotov cocktail)**
So until my following, more

magnificent job,

Where I will no doubt find more

cents to rob,

I hope that this heist,

Defines the zeitgeist,

And if this has sufficed,

I will take my leave,

Farm some leaves,

And this ne'er-do-well,

Bids thee farewell,

So I'll see you in hell,

Or at least in the sequel.

For I am Bad E. Man

And the E!

Stands!

For Evi-Gahhh!

[**Connor** who was sniffling throughout the entire monologue sneezes, shooting his **pistol** at **BadMan** interrupting his final words.]

Connor (irritated) Oh God not another one!

[**Richard** and **Alan** each stare at the lifeless **BadMan**, frozen as **Connor** pulls out his **Walkie Talkie. Scott** is also lying on the floor.]

Connor (non-chalant)	Sarge... yeah I shot another one... not this time... yes sir.**(hangs up)** Well my job here is done.

[**Connor** exits, lights go out for *Steps*.]

Richard (in disbelief)	He... He's... He's dead...
Alan (cautiously)	And we're... not?
Richard (confused)	But, the Molotov cocktail, he dropped it... we should be dead, lit up in an inferno.
Scott (proudly)	You're very welcome lads.
Alan	What the... Scott you're alive?
Scott	'Course I am, sure ya just heard me talkin'.
Richard	Well yes but... you got shot.
Alan	You gotta be dead by now

Scott I'll be alright.

Alan Well if ya say so.

Richard Just untie us, already.

Scott Say please poshy.

Richard Please poshy.

Scott S'pose that's the best I'm gonna get.

[**Scott** unties the pair. The three of them stand up to leave, speaking dryly as if in a mundane situation.]

Richard So... how did we not die?

Scott I drank the Molotov cocktail.

Alan Shouldn't that hurt?

Scott Wee bit of heartburn, yeah.

Richard Are you going to go to the hospital for that shoulder wound?

Scott Not allowed.

Alan Why?

Scott Not allowed in hospitals any more.

Richard Why not?

Scott Sucked all the ethanol out of those pad things they use to stay drunk.

Richard	Oh...
Alan	So you're just gonna die then?
Scott	Nope. Sucking out all the ethanol allowed me to absorb it's healin' properties, this'll take two days to heal, at worst three. In the meantime I think I'll go break in the new drinkin' arm.
Richard	Well hang on now, surely we can't just leave, we must be complacent in something.
Scott	I think ya mean complicit but no, not really, you didn't do anything that bad, the cameras would've picked up we were hostages, so the polis won't really blame us for holdin' the money for a minute, that's all we really did.
Richard	I suppose so... but weren't you the getaway driver?

Scott	I never even drove the car, if anythin' I'm the hero, I phoned the polis, never even touched the money, never shot anyone, I freed the hostages, and I stopped the building from blowin'.
Richard	But hang on, Alaan killed a man.
Alan (offended)	That is not true! I killed a Canadian.
Richard	So we really just leave then?
Scott	Aye, I'm getting' a drink, wouldn't want to sober up now.
Richard	Well I guess we'll see each other soon.
Alan	Actually I doubt that. I'm goin' back to the south, Vermont sucks.
Richard	I guess I'll be off doing... posh things.

[**Richard**, **Scott** and **Alan e**ach exit *Stage Right.* The lights go completely out and the curtains begin to close, before they fully close.]

The Director Hello? Anyone here?

(dour)

[Curtains pull back and the lights come back on. **The Director** enters *Stage Right.*]

The Director The customer service here is awful, I just want to get a lo-

[**The Director** seemingly notices **BadMan** on the floor and pauses for a moment.]

The Director Lo and behold, fortune shines upon

(walking) me. Oooh a dollar, oooh a dollar. Oooh a bag containing twenty three million dollars.

[**The Director** picks up the **burlap sacks**, completely missing **BadMan**, walking towards *Stage Left* picking up individual dollars on his way, eventually making a full circle and exiting *Stage Right.*]

BadMan **(roaring awake)** Evil!

[**BadMan** wakes up violently and sits up quickly.]

BadMan That's the last time I buy a used bullet proof vest, "acceptable condition" yeah right, well it got the job done. Now to take my cash and go.

[**BadMan** goes to grab the **burlap sacks** only to realise they are no longer there.]

BadMan Oh well, I guess I'll just try again in the sequel.

[**BadMan** laughs maniacally as the curtains close.]

The End

Thank You For Your (bad) Performances

Joshua "Badman*" Todd	**Original BadMan**
Sam Reid	**Original Scott**
	Original Ken
	Original Donald
Aaron Gallagher	**Original Alan**
Sebastian O'Hagan John	**Original Richard**
Frank Stewart	
Greg Stanage	**Original Director**
	Original Connor

*Joshua insisted that BadMan be spelt wrong in this instance

Extra Bad thanks to

LibreOffice Writer – For being better than a certain other free writing software that rhymes with "Schmoogal Schmocs".

Documan Medium – For Not Needing a License.

AvenirNext Lt Pro Regular – For Not Needing a License.

Gill Sans Ultra Bold – For Not Needing a License.

Printed in Great Britain
by Amazon